$16.99
ocn794821315
1st ed.   07/31/2012

I GOTTA DRAW

Bruce Degen

HARPER

An Imprint of HarperCollinsPublishers

Library of Congress Cataloging-in-Publication Data

Degen, Bruce.

    I gotta draw. — 1st ed.

        p.   cm.

    Summary: Elementary school student Charlie Muttnik loves to draw so much that it interferes with his schoolwork, until his teacher comes up with a creative solution.

    ISBN 978-0-06-028417-6 (trade bdg.) — ISBN 978-0-06-028418-3 (lib. bdg.)

    [1. Drawing—Fiction.   2. Schools—Fiction.   3. Ability—Fiction.   4. Dogs—Fiction.]   I. Title.

PZ7.D3635Ch 2012   2011010033

[E]—dc22   CIP

                                                               AC

12 13 14 15 16 SCP 10 9 8 7 6 5 4 3 2 1

❖

First Edition

IN MEMORY OF RENEE DARVIN
With a passion for excellence and a wildly generous heart,
to grateful students, rising young artists, inspired teachers, loving friends,
she was a great wave. She swept us all up,
and we would find ourselves set down, surprised, in new places.
—BD

Hey! I'm Charlie Muttnik.
Everyone on the block knows me.
I am the pup with the pencil,
the mutt with the marker,
the dog with the drawing pad,
the chap with the chalk!
I'm drawing all the time.
And as soon as I finish one drawing—
I gotta draw another!

Why am I drawing all the time?
I don't know, but it's all I want to do.
My drawing might start out as a butterfly
and end up as a battleship.
It could turn out funny,
or strange, or cool . . .
or maybe . . . just a mess.
I don't mind.
I take a fresh piece of paper. . . .
I feel a little shiver. . . .
Something new is about to happen . . .
and I'm off again!

Sometimes it seems there is no place at all.

So I go outside.
There are always kids in the street.

I see Stanley . . . and Melvin . . . and Ira.

We draw a skelly court on the sidewalk.
In the center I draw a skull in white chalk.

When you're a kid, there's no escape. Summer ends, and you gotta go to school. It's the *law*.

She is busy doing all this stuff at her desk.
I'd like to take out my pencil and draw, but I better ask nicely.
I raise my hand and call out, in a friendly way.

HEY, TEACHER!

HAY IS FOR HORSES, NOT FOR TEACHERS. YOU MUST SAY, "EXCUSE ME, MISS RICH." WE ARE IN SCHOOL, NOT IN A STABLE.

And she gives me a look . . . a look you might give to chewing gum stuck to the bottom of your shoe.

But there is <u>not</u> a lot
of drawing.
And I gotta draw.
So, as usual, my pencil finds
all kinds of places
that could use a little
<u>creative</u> attention.

Miss Rich is beginning to
notice that I like to draw.
But not in a good way.

She is annoyed.

She is exasperated.

My report card never makes it
to the beginning of the alphabet.
No A's.
Some C's.
And two red F's
for <u>Neatness</u> and <u>Cooperation</u>.

I REMEMBER YOUR SISTER.
SHE WAS A GOOD STUDENT.
WHAT HAPPENED WITH YOU?

On Parents' Night my mother and father
go to school to talk to Miss Rich.
When they come home, my mother is wailing.
My father is growling.

IT'S A DISGRACE!

IT'S A DISASTER!

NO TV FOR A MONTH!

NO MOVIES!

NO ICE CREAM!

NO SLEEPING!

NO BREATHING!

NO NOTHING!

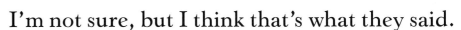

I'm not sure, but I think that's what they said.

I am working on my report on <u>climate</u>.
I need to get an A on this or I may
never see a TV show again.
Making notes is <u>so boring</u>!
So I draw penguins, and palm trees,
like in the climate books.

When I hand it in, Miss Rich sighs
and rolls her eyes to the ceiling.
I don't know what she is looking for up there,
but I bet it's not an <u>A+</u> for me.

Uh-oh. What does that mean?

The next day Miss Rich calls me to the back of the classroom.
She tapes some paper to the blackboard.
She says I can stand there and draw while the class
is working on our spelling list.
WOW!
I draw a picture of Stanley playing stoopball.
I'm feeling pretty good!

I draw an aardvark
playing stoopball with Stanley,
and I hear myself say out loud...

I think of Old Yonah in his little store
with the pickles and sauerkraut in big barrels,
and I draw a kid fishing out a sour pickle,
the kind that makes your mouth water.

I'm right again!
I draw and spell at the back of
the room till we finish the list . . .
and believe it or not,
I can spell almost all the words.

A couple of days later,
Miss Rich brings out a set
of poster paints and brushes.

PAINTING SMOCKS

SUPPLIES

Wow! I <u>never</u> get to paint at home.
My mother says paints are too messy
in a small apartment!
I pour some of each color
and I try mixing colors together.
Cool!

Miss Rich says I can paint while we do
social studies if I can name the
five boroughs of New York City.

I paint a picture of my grandpa
in his garden with his watering can
and the sun shining down and
the crazy flowers jammed in between
the fences and the brick walls
in our little backyard in Brooklyn.

And so I get to paint a lot.

I read that in our history book!
I paint old Henry and me
sailing up his river.
I call it the MUTTNIK RIVER.

I remember the library book about space.
I paint me, the E.T.T.—
        Extra-Terrestrial Terrier—
            visiting all the planets.

I looked it up in the encyclopedia!
I paint a "corny" picture . . . with a frame
exactly in the shape of Iowa.

Maybe school isn't so bad—
when you're painting.
My report card is beginning to meet up
with the beginning of the alphabet.
And there are no red F's.

Miss Rich is looking at all my artwork.
She gets a weird new expression on her face.
What is it? Could you call that a smile?

CHILDREN, PERHAPS _EVERYBODY_ IN OUR CLASS CAN PAINT AND SPELL.

Everybody comes to see our show.
My mother and father and sister,
and the other kids' families,
and lots of other folks, too.

A lady with a very interesting hat walks in.
It turns out she is a famous artist.
Principal Bowser shows her around.
She looks at every picture
with her head tilted this way and that.

Then she hangs a BLUE RIBBON on mine!

That's how I won my first blue ribbon . . .

and got my best report card . . .

and a special place to draw . . .

'cause, you know . . . I GOTTA draw!